ROCKFORD PUBLIC LIBRARY

3 1112 01570908 8

W9-AOP-172

E MCC
McCann, Dan
Balloon on the moon

051908

WITHDRAWN

ROCKFORD PUBLIC LIBRARY

Rockford, Illinois

www.rockfordpubliclibrary.org

815-965-9511

BALLOON ON THE MOON

Dan McCann
Illustrated by Nathan Hale

Walker & Company New York

ROCKFORD PUBLIC LIBRARY

To Jake, Will & Lizzie—my inspirations;
to Sharon—my hero;
to Kelly—my everything
—D. M.

To Pluto, we hardly knew you
—N. H.

Text copyright © 2008 by Dan McCann
Illustrations copyright © 2008 by Nathan Hale

All rights reserved. No part of this book may be reproduced or transmitted in any form or by any means,
electronic or mechanical, including photocopying, recording, or by any information storage
and retrieval system, without permission in writing from the publisher.

First published in the United States of America in 2008 by Walker Publishing Company, Inc.
Distributed to the trade by Macmillan

For information about permission to reproduce selections from this book, write to
Permissions, Walker & Company, 175 Fifth Avenue, New York, New York 10010

Library of Congress Cataloging-in-Publication Data
McCann, Dan.
Balloon on the moon / by Dan McCann ; illustrated by Nathan Hale.
p.   cm.
Summary: When his little brother's red balloon goes flying off into the sky, six-and-three-quarters-year-old
Jake goes on a mission to the moon to retrieve it for him, because that is what big brothers are for.
ISBN-13: 978-0-8027-8092-8 • ISBN-10: 0-8027-8092-X (hardcover)
ISBN-13: 978-0-8027-8093-5 • ISBN-10: 0-8027-8093-8 (reinforced)
[1. Brothers—Fiction. 2. Balloons—Fiction. 3. Lost and found possessions—Fiction.
4. Space flight to the moon—Fiction.] I. Hale, Nathan, ill. II. Title.
PZ7.M1241Bal 2008   [E]—dc22   2007032180

Typeset in ITC Bauhaus Medium
The art for this book was created using Golden Acrylics on Crescent board and Adobe Photoshop.

Visit Walker & Company's Web site at www.walkeryoungreaders.com

Printed in Malaysia
2 4 6 8 10 9 7 5 3 1 (hardcover)
2 4 6 8 10 9 7 5 3 1 (reinforced)

All papers used by Walker & Company are natural, recyclable products
made from wood grown in well-managed forests. The manufacturing processes
conform to the environmental regulations of the country of origin.

Daddy was quick but not quick enough. A gust of wind caught Will's red balloon and swept it skyward. Daddy jumped for the string, but it was no use.

Soon the balloon was off, off, off—nothing but a small red dot in the clear blue sky.

"I'm sorry, Will," said Daddy. "It looks like it's off to the moon."

Will started to cry, which made Jake, his big brother, very sad.

Lying in his bed that night, Jake thought about how much Will loved that balloon. Just before he dozed off, a wild idea came to him. Yes, he decided that's what he had to do.

Accomplishing this most important mission required a trip to the Kennedy Space Center, NASA's launch headquarters. While his mom looked at a rocket model, Jake headed for the front counter.

"One ticket to the moon, please," he said politely.

"How old are you?" asked the woman behind the counter.

"I'm six and three-quarters," said Jake proudly.

"Just a minute," said the woman. She picked up the phone and spoke in a whisper. Moments later, a man in a dark blue suit came out.

"So," said the man in the dark blue suit, "I hear you want to be an astronaut."

"My brother's balloon flew to the moon," said Jake. "I'm going to get it for him."

The man in the dark blue suit looked hard at the boy.

"I won't take up much space," Jake continued. "I don't even have to eat. Well, maybe just a snack or two..."

"You've got spunk," the man replied. "I like that. The next mission leaves tomorrow at eight."

"I'll be there," said Jake with a smile, "as long as my mom and dad say it's okay."

"Of course," said the man in the dark blue suit. "Welcome aboard . . . as long as your mom and dad say it's okay."

Jake's mom and dad really weren't too thrilled with the idea of their oldest son hurtling through space—especially since he was only six and three-quarters. But they agreed when they saw how sad Will was without his red balloon and how determined Jake was to help.

Jake was back at the space center at seven o'clock sharp the next morning. A mob of reporters and photographers was there, asking question after question.

"Are you nervous?"

"Do you like Tang?"

"Shouldn't you be in school?"

The time came for Jake to say good-bye to his family.

"Let's get you suited up," said the man in dark blue.

A team of men and women put Jake into his specially fitted space suit. They slid his hands into special gloves and snapped on his helmet.

Inside the rocket, a booster seat was waiting. The crew strapped Jake in tightly. His nervous stomach was doing flips. To make matters worse, he had forgotten to go to the bathroom. It was too late now.

4

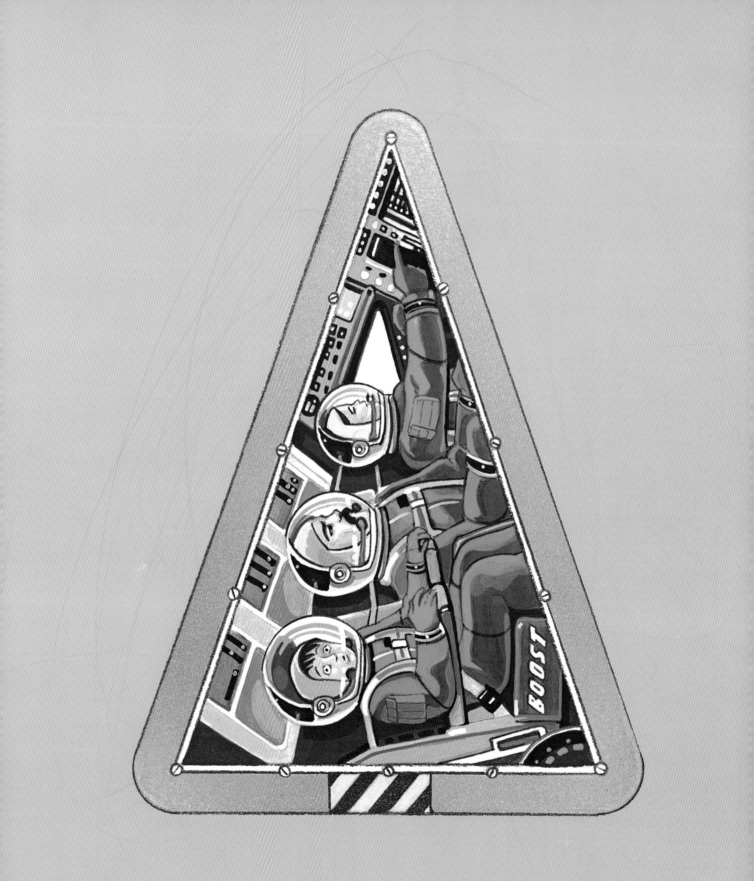

"Let's go get that red balloon," said the commander.

The booster rockets roared to life.

"Godspeed, Jake," said a voice from mission control.

On went the countdown:

three...

two...

one...

BLASTOFF!

"Bye-bye, Jake," Will yelled from below.

The engines were loud. The ride was bumpy—bumpier than any roller coaster.

"How are you doing, Jake?" asked the commander as they shot spaceward.

"Can't talk," he replied, trying hard not to toss his cookies.

Jake grabbed his armrests and took a deep breath. Then, before he knew it, the bumping stopped. The rocket had arrived in outer space.

His cookies intact, Jake unfastened his seat belt and slipped off his helmet. It began to float . . . and so did he.

"Whoa," said Jake quietly, "I'm flying."

Excitement erupted as he "swam" to the window.

"I'm flying, oh yeah! I'm flying, oh yeah!"

Jake did a few flips on the way, then he stopped
to gaze outside. What an amazing view!

"Is that . . . ," he began.

"That's Mother Earth," said the commander.
"That's where we live—and where the people who
love us live."

Jake's smile melted away. Suddenly he missed his mom, dad, and brother. He missed his bedroom and his toys. He had to remind himself he was on a mission—a most important one.

"You must be hungry," said the commander.

Jake remembered saying that he wouldn't eat anything, but he was starving. He gobbled up a hot dog, which was pretty cold, and some astronaut ice cream, which wasn't. He washed it all down with a pouch of Tang.

After dinner, Jake drifted into a peaceful sleep. Making history can be tiring, especially when you have to wake up at six o'clock in the morning to do it.

By the time Jake woke, the rocket was orbiting the moon.

"Jake!" called the commander. "It's time."

The boy astronaut made his way to the lunar module, which, after a quick descent, landed softly on the moon.

"You are 'Go' for moonwalk," said mission control. "Good luck, Jake."

Jake carefully climbed down the ladder and onto the lunar surface.

"That's one small step for a little man," said Jake, "one giant leap for childkind."

Jake looked around. It was so quiet. He squinted his eyes, and there, tangled among some moon rocks, he saw it—his brother's red balloon, along with a collection of wayward kites and some other lost toys. His stomach jumped with excitement.

"I'm going for capture," said Jake.

He bounced over to the rocks and swiftly
snagged Will's balloon. He grabbed a couple of
kites as well.
   "Someone on Earth is probably missing you."
   Jake planted an American flag in the soil and
wrote a "J" and a "W" with his gloved finger.
Then he made his way back to the lunar module—
mission accomplished.

The crew let out a great cheer.

"Hooray for Jake!" they shouted.

"Mission control," said the commander, "we're coming home."

"Can we swing by the North Pole?" asked Jake.

"Negative," said the commander.

The reentry into Earth's atmosphere was no picnic. Jake was very hot in his flight suit, and his stomach was queasy. But the splashdown was perfect.

After the helicopter brought Jake in, the reporters and photographers were waiting.

"Did you see any moon people?"

"How does it feel to be the youngest astronaut in history?"

"Did you toss your cookies?"

Most important, they asked, "Did you find your brother's balloon?"

Jake proudly held it up for the crowd to see.

NJH076

Jake was happy to have met so many nice people, happy to have flown into orbit, and happy to have walked on the moon. But seeing his brother's face when he brought back his red balloon—that made him happiest of all.

"Thank you, Jake," said Will.

"You're welcome, Will," said Jake. "That's what big brothers are for."